My Weirder-est School #3

Dr. Floss Is the Boss!

Dan Gutman

Pictures by
Jim Paillot

HARPER

An Imprint of HarperCollinsPublishers

To the kids at Cos Cob School

Special thanks to Jeannie Schnakenberg, Tanabe Yamagishi Yuka, and Cassandra Tai-Marcellini

My Weirder-est School #3: Dr. Floss Is the Boss!
Text copyright © 2019 by Dan Gutman
Illustrations copyright © 2019 by Jim Paillot
information address HarperCollins Children's Books, a division of HarperCollins Publishers, 195 Broadway, New York, NY 10007.
www.harpercollinschildrens.com

ISBN 978-0-06-269107-1 (pbk. bdg.)—ISBN 978-0-06-269108-8 (library bdg.)

Typography by Laura Mock
19 20 21 22 23   PC/BRR   10 9 8 7 6 5 4 3 2
❖
First Edition

Contents

1. National Dessert Day   1

2. Betsy Toothbrush   10

3. Molar Monkey   23

4. Our Genius Plan   36

5. Plaque Attack!   47

6. The Tooth Fairy   58

7. Open Wide and Say Ah!   68

8. Good News and Bad News   80

9. Swish and Spit   96

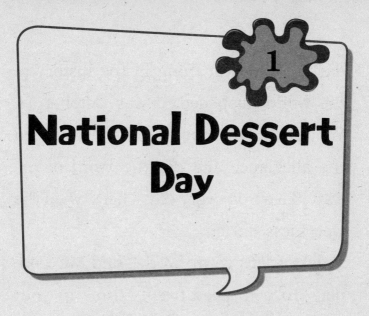

National Dessert Day

My name is A.J. and I hate going to the dentist.

Dentists are weird. Why would anybody want to be a dentist? Who wants to stick their hands in people's mouths all day long? That's just gross.

I only mention this because the other

day the weirdest thing in the history of the world happened. It was October 14. We were in Mr. Cooper's class. We pledged the allegiance and did the Word of the Day, like we do every day. That's when the weirdness started.

"Okay, let's get to work," said Mr. Cooper. "Turn to page twenty-three in your math books."

Ugh. I hate math. But that's when a voice came over the loudspeaker. It was Mrs. Patty, the school secretary.

"Attention, students in Mr. Cooper's class . . ." she announced.

"Not again," muttered Mr. Cooper.

". . . please report to Mrs. Cooney's office."

Mrs. Cooney is our school nurse. She has blue eyes that look like cotton candy yogurt. The kind with no sprinkles. One time, she begged me to marry her, but I told her I couldn't because she was already married to some guy named Mr. Cooney.

"Pringle up, everybody," said Mr. Cooper.

We all lined up, like Pringles. Everybody was wondering why we were going to the nurse's office.

"Mrs. Cooney is probably going to check to see if we have head lice," said Andrea Young, this annoying girl with curly brown hair.

"Headlights?" I said. "I don't have headlights."

"Why would we bring headlights to school?" asked Ryan, who will eat anything, even stuff that isn't food.

"I don't think headlights would fit in my backpack," said Michael, who never ties his shoes.

"You could bring two backpacks," suggested Alexia, this girl who rides a skateboard all the time. "One for each headlight."

"How would you get the headlights off a car?" asked Neil, who we call the nude kid even though he wears clothes.

"Not headlights, you dumbheads!" shouted Andrea. *"Head lice!"*

Oh. Those words sound way too much alike.*

"Maybe Mrs. Cooney is going to weigh and measure us," guessed Emily, Andrea's crybaby friend. "She does that every year."

We walked a million hundred miles to the nurse's office. Alexia was the line leader. Ryan was the door holder.

"Good morning, boys and girls!" said

_____

* Ha-ha! Made you look down!

6

Mrs. Cooney as we filed into her office.

As I walked by her, I whispered to Mrs. Cooney, "I just want you to know that I don't have headlights."

"Good to know, A.J.," she replied.

We sat down on long benches. I had to sit next to annoying Andrea.

"Are you going to check us for head lice?" Andrea asked.

"No," said Mrs. Cooney.

"Are you going to weigh and measure us?" asked Emily.

"No," said Mrs. Cooney. "How many of you like going to the dentist?"

Andrea raised her hand. She was waving it in the air like she was stranded on a desert island, trying to signal a plane.

"I *love* going to the dentist," she said. "I go every six months."

"Me too!" said Emily, who does everything Andrea does.

"I *hate* going to the dentist," I announced.

"Me too," everybody else said.

"Well, you kids are in luck," said Mrs.

Cooney, "because you don't have to go to the dentist today. The dentist is coming to *you*!"

WHAT?!

"Today is National Dessert Day," said Mrs. Cooney. "So I thought it would be the *perfect* day to bring in a dentist to visit our school. I'd like to introduce you to . . . Dr. Floss!"

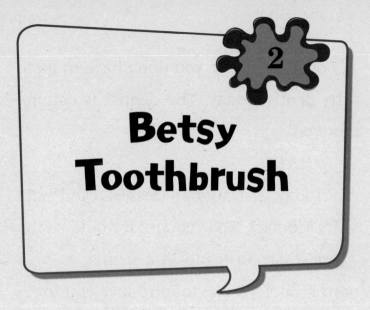

Betsy Toothbrush

This lady walked into the nurse's office. She was wearing a white coat, the kind that doctors wear. There was a name tag on it that said "Dr. Betsy Floss." We gave her a round of applause by clapping our hands in circles, because that's what you're supposed to do whenever somebody is introduced. Nobody knows why.

"Happy National Dessert Day!" she said.
"You all have such nice smiles. Look at all
the things your teeth do for you. You see
them when you smile. You use them to
chew your food. They help you talk and
sing, whisper, and whistle. It's nice to see
your smiling faces this morning. My name
is Betsy Floss."

"Didn't Betsy Floss make the first flag?" I whispered to Andrea.

"That was Betsy *Ross*, dumbhead," she whispered back.

I was going to say something mean to Andrea, but I didn't have the chance.

"Is Betsy Floss your *real* name?" asked Ryan.

"Well, I took my husband's name when I got married," Dr. Floss told us. "His last name is Floss."

"What name were you born with?" asked Emily.

"Betsy Toothbrush," replied Dr. Floss.

"Wait," I said. "Your last name was Toothbrush and you married a guy named Floss?"

"Yes."

"Is your husband a dentist too?" asked Neil.

"No, of course not," replied Dr. Floss. "Why would you think that?"

"It was just a guess," said Neil.

Mrs. Cooney took a step forward. "Tell us a little about yourself, Dr. Floss," she said. "What made you decide to go into the field of dentistry?"

"Well, let me think," said Dr. Floss. "I used to be in the army."

"What did you do in the army?" asked Michael.

"I was a drill sergeant," she replied, and then she started cracking up. "Get it? Drill sergeant? Ha-ha-ha. That's a little dentist joke."

Everybody pretended to laugh even though she didn't say anything funny. When grown-ups tell jokes, you should always pretend to laugh. That's the first rule of being a kid.

"When I got out of the army," continued Dr. Floss, "I decided to go to dental school. I've been practicing dentistry for ten years."

"Don't you get tired?" I asked.

"Ha-ha-ha. I get it," said Dr. Floss. "Any other questions?"

"What do you do when you're not being a dentist?" asked Neil.

"Let me see," said Dr. Floss. "I like to work with my hands. I play guitar. I collect old tools. I walk my dog. And I like to do roadwork."

"You work on the roads?" I asked.

"I think roadwork means she goes jogging, Arlo," whispered Andrea, who calls me by my real name because she knows I don't like it.

"Did you kids lose any of your baby teeth yet?" asked Dr. Floss.

Most of us raised our hands.

"I have a loose tooth right now," said Emily.

"Oooh!" said Dr. Floss. "Maybe it will fall out today, and if you're lucky the Tooth Fairy will come to school. She's a good friend of mine."

"We invited Dr. Floss here today to talk

about dental hygiene," said Mrs. Cooney. "Who can tell me what hygiene is?"

"That's when you say hello to somebody named Jean," I said.

Andrea rolled her eyes and shot her hand in the air.

"Hygiene is all the things we do to stay healthy," she said.

"That's right, Andrea," said Mrs. Cooney.

Andrea smiled the smile she smiles to let everybody know she knows something nobody else knows.

"Our students have been taught all about good hygiene, Dr. Floss," said Mrs. Cooney. "They know they should brush their teeth at least twice a day."

"I brush my teeth *seven* times a day," said

Andrea. "First I brush when I wake up in the morning. Then I brush after breakfast. Before lunch. After lunch. Before dinner. After dinner. And at bedtime. I have a tooth-brushing calendar in my room. I put a check mark after every time I brush."

"Can you possibly be more boring?" I asked Andrea.

What is her problem? Why can't a truck full of toothpaste fall on her head?

"Kids should also eat a healthy diet for the sake of their teeth," said Mrs. Cooney. "Isn't that right, Dr. Floss?"

"No," replied Dr. Floss.

"HUH?" we all said, which is also "HUH" backward.

"I wish kids would *never* brush their

teeth or eat healthy," said Dr. Floss. "If you all brush your teeth regularly and eat healthy food, there will be no need for dentists. I want kids to *stop* brushing their teeth, eat more candy and cupcakes, and drink sugary sodas."

WHAT?!

"I don't understand," said Mrs. Cooney. "You're saying you want kids to have poor dental hygiene because it would be good for your business?"

"Exactly!" said Dr. Floss. "You see, my car is old and it keeps breaking down. If kids have good dental hygiene, they won't need to visit the dentist very often, and I won't make much money. I want you kids to eat *more* sugary junk food, so I can buy a new car."

"WOW!" we all said, which is "MOM" upside down. That was weird.

"October is my favorite month of the year," said Dr. Floss. "I'll tell you why.

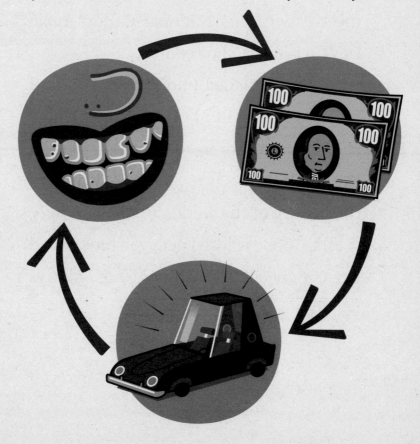

October eighteenth is National Chocolate Cupcake Day. The twenty-third is National Boston Cream Pie Day. The twenty-fifth is National Greasy Foods Day. The twenty-eighth is National Chocolate Day. The thirtieth is National Candy Corn Day. And the thirty-first is National Candy Apple Day.* It's also Halloween!"

Dr. Floss reached into her pockets and pulled out a handful of candy. She threw it up in the air for us to catch. I grabbed a Kit Kat. Dr. Floss is my favorite dentist in the history of the world.

Mrs. Cooney closed her eyes and rubbed her forehead. Grown-ups are always

---

* Look 'em up if you don't believe me.

rubbing their forehead. Nobody knows why.

"I'd love to talk more about dental hygiene," said Dr. Floss, "but I have to go say hello to the other classes."

"No! Don't go!" everybody was hollering.

"We want more candy!"

"I'll be back," said Dr. Floss. "We'll be celebrating National Dessert Day all day."

Yay! This was going to be the greatest day of my life.

Molar Monkey

We left the nurse's office and walked a million hundred miles back to our classroom.

"Okay, turn to page twenty-three in your math books," Mr. Cooper told us.

Math was boring. Why do we need math when we have calculators? Luckily, we didn't have the chance to finish the lesson, because you'll never believe who walked through the door.

Nobody! You can't walk through a door. Doors are made out of wood. But you'll never believe who walked through the door*way*. It was Dr. Floss! This time, she was carrying a guitar.

"Yay! It's Dr. Floss!" everybody was shouting. "More candy!"

Mr. Cooper closed his eyes and rubbed his forehead. I guess when you get older, your forehead gets itchy a lot.

"Would you kids like to hear a song?" asked Dr. Floss.

"Yes!" shouted all the girls.

"No!" shouted all the boys.

Anytime anybody asks you if you want to hear a song, always say no. That's the first rule of being a boy.

"This is a song called 'My Favorite Things,'" said Dr. Floss. She strummed her guitar and started to sing . . .

Snickers and Kit Kats
and ten Almond Joys.
Cookies and sodas
for girls and for boys.
Milk Duds and gumballs,
a box of Ring Dings.
These are a few of my favorite things.

Ice cream and candy
and cakes filled with sugar.
It's fine with me if you
eat your own boogers.
Skittles and Hershey's
and one Nestlé Crunch.
These are the things
that I want you to munch.

When you get sick,

if you feel ick,

and think you're gonna die,

just eat lots more junk food

that rots lots more teeth,

'cause there's stuff I need . . . to buy.

That song was weird. Mr. Cooper rubbed his forehead again. He really needs to use moisturizer.

"I think Dr. Floss is just joking," he told us. "She doesn't *really* want kids to eat lots of junk food. Do you, Dr. Floss?"

But Dr. Floss wasn't paying attention. She put down her guitar and picked up a weird-looking puppet. It was a monkey puppet with a big mouth full of teeth. The monkey's hands were up in the air like somebody was robbing it. Dr. Floss's hand was inside the back of the puppet to make its mouth move.

"Hi boys and girls," the monkey puppet said in a squeaky voice. "My name is Molar. Molar Monkey. And this is my friend Dr. Floss."

Dr. Floss was trying not to move her mouth when the monkey spoke, but it was obvious that she was doing the talking.

"Hi Molar!" said Dr. Floss in her regular voice.

"We're going to talk about teeth," said Molar Monkey. "But first, a few jokes."

"I like jokes," said Dr. Floss.

"Did you hear about the cell phone that went to the dentist?" Molar Monkey asked us.

"No, I didn't," said Dr. Floss. "What about it?"

"It had Bluetooth," said Molar Monkey. "Get it? Blue . . . tooth?"

Everybody laughed even though the monkey puppet didn't say anything funny.

"Hey, do you know why kids don't like going to the dentist?" Molar Monkey asked us.

"No, why?" asked Dr. Floss.

"Because dentists are boring," said Molar Monkey. "Get it? Boring?"

I didn't get it, but I laughed anyway. You should always laugh after a monkey puppet tells a joke. That's the first rule of being a kid.

"Okay, enough with the jokes," said Molar Monkey. "When you brush your teeth blah blah blah blah back teeth blah blah blah blah front teeth blah blah blah blah tops and bottoms blah blah blah blah and don't forget to brush your tongue blah blah blah blah . . ."

What a snoozefest. Molar Monkey was right. Dentists *are* boring. And so are their puppets.

"Do monkeys even brush their teeth?" I whispered to Ryan.

"Not that I know of," Ryan whispered back.

"Then why is he telling us to brush

ours?" I whispered.

"Why is that monkey even speaking English?" whispered Ryan. "Monkeys can't talk."

". . . blah blah blah blah," continued Molar Monkey. "You don't have to brush *all* your teeth. Only brush the ones you want to keep. Ha-ha. That's a little dental joke there."

Molar Monkey took about a million hundred hours to explain how to brush our teeth. Like we didn't know that already!

"We should talk about flossing now," said Dr. Floss. "Who knows how to use dental floss?"

"I do!" shouted Little Miss Perfect I

Know Everything in the World. "I've been flossing since I was four years old."

"Don't you get tired?" I asked.

Anytime somebody says they've been doing something for years, ask them if they don't get tired. That's the first rule of being a kid.

"Very funny, Arlo," Andrea said, rolling her eyes.

"Flossing cleans between your teeth where food can hide and your toothbrush can't reach," said Molar Monkey.

"So you kids should *never* use dental floss," said Dr. Floss. "Because if you don't, the food will stay in there and cause holes in your teeth called cavities. And when you have cavities, you'll have to come to the dentist, and your parents will have to pay me lots of money. And then I can buy my new car."

"That's a horrible attitude, Dr. Floss!" said Molar Monkey.

"Hey, I'm just looking out for number one," said Dr. Floss.*

"Just ignore her," said Molar Monkey. "Flossing your teeth is a really good thing. I'm going to give each of you some dental floss so you can use it at home."

Molar Monkey showed us how to use dental floss and gave each of us a little

---

* Gross! I'm just glad she's not looking out for number two.

container of it. Yay! I love getting free stuff.

"Dental floss comes in lots of flavors," said Molar Monkey. "My favorite is mint. Remember, you kids should floss every day."

"They should not," said Dr. Floss.

"They should too," said Molar Monkey.

"Should not," said Dr. Floss. "I need a new car."

They went on like that for a while.

Our Genius Plan

After lunch in the vomitorium, we went out for recess. Michael's birthday was last week, and we were all playing with the yo-yos we got in our goody bags at the end of the party. Yo-yos are cool.

Emily was looking worried, as usual.

"I think my tooth is going to fall out

soon," she said. "It's really loose."

What's up with baby teeth? Why do we have baby teeth if they're just going to fall out and get replaced by adult teeth? We should just *start* with adult teeth and get it over with, if you ask me. Having two sets of teeth makes no sense at all. What a waste of teeth.

"Maybe we should tell Dr. Floss that your tooth is about to fall out," Andrea told Emily.

"I'm scared," said Emily, who's scared of everything.

"That's a terrible idea," I said. "Dr. Floss is weird. I don't even think she's a real dentist. A real dentist would never tell kids to eat junk food."

"Maybe Dr. Floss kidnapped the *real* dentist who was supposed to visit our school," said Ryan.

"Yeah," I said, "the real dentist is probably tied to some railroad tracks right now, and a train is coming. Stuff like that happens all the time, you know."

"Stop trying to scare Emily," said Andrea.

"I'm scared," repeated Emily. "I'm afraid my tooth is going to fall out any minute. I can feel it with my tongue."

"I'm going to go get Dr. Floss," Andrea said, and then she went running into the school.

"Do you think Dr. Floss is going to pull out my loose tooth?" Emily asked us.

"Sure," I told her. "That's what dentists do. They love it when kids have loose teeth."

"Your parents are going to have to pay Dr. Floss a lot of money to pull out that tooth," Neil told Emily.

"How much do you think it will cost?" asked Emily.

"I don't know," said Ryan. "How much does a car cost?"

"About a million dollars," I guessed.

I have no idea how much a car costs, but I know they cost a lot of money.

"What a scam," said Alexia. "If you don't do anything, your loose tooth will just fall out on its own at some point."

That's when I got a great idea.

"You don't need Dr. Floss, you know," I told Emily. "We can pull out that loose tooth for you."

"You can?"

"Sure," I said, unrolling my yo-yo. "Look. We can just put the loop at the end of this string around your loose tooth, give the yo-yo a good yank, and your tooth will pop right out."

"Are you sure?" asked Emily. She looked
nervous.

"Sure I'm sure," I said. "Easy peasy. And you won't have to pay Dr. Floss a dime."

"What a great idea!" said Alexia. "A.J., you should get the Nobel Prize."

That's a prize they give out to people who don't have bells.

"Well, okay I guess," said Emily.

Alexia tried to put the loop of the yo-yo string around Emily's loose tooth. She was struggling with it.*

"The yo-yo string is too thick," Alexia said. "The loop won't fit around the tooth."

Hmmm. Every problem has a solution. That's what my parents always tell me. And that's when I got the greatest idea in

---

* Kids, don't try this at home. We're professionals.

the history of the world.

"Dental floss!" I shouted.

I took the dental floss that Molar Monkey gave me out of my pocket and unspooled it. It stretched all the way to the swing set. Alexia tied one end of the dental floss to Emily's loose tooth. Dental floss is much thinner than yo-yo string, so it slipped right on.

"Hey, I have an idea," said Ryan. "Why don't we tie the other end of the dental floss to a swing and have somebody sit on the swing? When they swing forward, it'll pull out the tooth."

"You're a genius!" said Michael.

Ryan should really be in the gifted and

talented program. He tied the end of the dental floss to the swing. Alexia climbed onto the swing. We moved Emily behind the swing so there was just a little slack on the dental floss.

"I'm scared," said Emily.

"There's nothing to worry about," I assured her. "This is the same thing Dr. Floss would do. But we're doing it for free. Is everybody ready?"

"Ready!" everybody shouted.

"Open your mouth, Emily!" shouted Neil.

Emily opened her mouth.

"On your mark!" I shouted. "Get set! SWING!"

Alexia picked up her feet and swung forward. The line of dental floss got tight. Then something went flying out of Emily's mouth.

"Ahhhhhhhhhhh!" Emily shouted. "My tooth fell out!"

"Of *course* your tooth fell out," I told her. "That's what it was *supposed* to do."

You should have *been* there! We all clapped because our genius plan had worked perfectly. But Emily was yelling and screaming and hooting and hollering and freaking out.

"I've got to *do* something!" she yelled, and then she went running into the school.

Sheesh! Get a grip! What a crybaby.

Plaque Attack!

I thought we might get in trouble for pulling out Emily's tooth. But when we went back to Mr. Cooper's class after recess, nobody said a word. Emily and Andrea were just sitting there with their hands folded, like always.

"Okay, we wasted the whole morning,

so now it's time to get to work," said Mr. Cooper. "Turn to page twenty-three in your math books."

That's when the weirdest thing in the history of the world happened. Dr. Floss came running into the room. She wasn't wearing her dentist uniform anymore. She was dressed up in some weird super-hero costume with a big letter *P* on the front. And she had a dog with her.

"It is I," she announced, "the evil super-villain Captain Plaque! And this is my dog, Tartar!"

The dog barked.

"Cool!" we all shouted.

Mr. Cooper rubbed his forehead with

his fingers and closed his math book.

"Bwaaa-ha-ha!" shouted Dr. Floss in an evil supervillain voice. "Plaque has bacteria that grows when your food mixes with saliva in your mouth. It leads to cavities, and I *love* cavities. Isn't that right, Tartar?"

The dog barked again.

Tartar? Isn't that the stuff you put on fish sticks? I was going to say that, but then something even weirder happened. *Another* superhero came running into the room!

She was wearing a mask and she had a big letter *F* on the front of her uniform. Oh, and she was carrying a giant inflatable toothbrush.

"Oh no!" shouted Captain Plaque. "My archenemy is here!"

"Is it the Flash?" asked Ryan.

"No," said Captain Plaque.

"Is it one of the Fantastic Four?" asked Alexia.

"No," said Captain Plaque.

"It is I," announced the superhero with the *F* on her uniform. "Fluoride!

I fight a constant battle for good dental hygiene."

"Fluoride?" we all asked.

"Who can tell me what fluoride is?" asked Fluoride.

"Disney World is in Fluoride," I said.

"That's Florida, you dumbhead!" said Andrea. "Fluoride is a mineral that helps strengthen your teeth. It's in toothpaste."

"That's right!" said Fluoride.

Why can't a truck full of fluoride fall on Andrea's head?

If you ask me, that Fluoride lady sounded a lot like our librarian, Mrs. Roopy. She's always dressing up in weird costumes.

"Are you Mrs. Roopy in disguise?" I asked.

"Roopy?" said Fluoride. "Never heard of her. I'm Fluoride, nature's cavity fighter. Plaque is bad for you, and tartar is hard plaque that can grow on your teeth. It comes from the things you eat and drink. That's why it's so important to have a healthy diet to prevent cavities."

"Cavities are *good* things!" shouted Captain Plaque. "They give dentists lots of work so they can buy new cars. Isn't that right, Tartar?"

The dog barked.

"I thought tartar was that stuff you put on fish sticks," I said.

"That's tartar *sauce*, dumbhead!" said Andrea.

Those things should really have different names.

"Tartar and I are here to destroy your teeth," shouted Captain Plaque.

"Not if I can help it!" shouted Fluoride. "Stand back, kids!"

That's when the weirdest thing in the history of the world happened. Fluoride hit Captain Plaque over the head with her giant inflatable toothbrush! Then Captain Plaque karate-chopped Fluoride!

"It's time for another plaque attack!" shouted Captain Plaque.

"No!" shouted Fluoride. "Captain Plaque is wack!"

Watching the two of them fight was

cool. Meanwhile, Tartar just stood there, barking.

"I don't approve of all this violence," said Andrea. "It's a bad influence on children."

"What do you have against violins?" I asked.

"Not violins, Arlo! Violence!"

I was just yanking Andrea's chain. Captain Plaque and Fluoride were going at it pretty good. Finally Fluoride knocked Captain Plaque down with her giant toothbrush. Everybody cheered.

"Hit the road, Plaque," said Fluoride, "and don't you come back no more."*

Captain Plaque slinked out of the room

---

* Ask your parents to explain this. If they can't, ask your grandparents.

with Tartar, and we cheered some more. Fluoride gave each of us one of those little timers that have sand in them and told us we should always brush our teeth for two minutes.

"I will fight plaque and tartar wherever I find them," said Fluoride. "Farewell! I must take my leave."

Why would she take leaves? We don't even have any leaves to take. There's no tree in the classroom.

Fluoride took a bow and we all clapped again. Then she climbed out the window.

That was weird.

The Tooth Fairy

A few minutes later, Dr. Floss came back in the room. She wasn't dressed up like Captain Plaque anymore.

"I'd like to introduce a surprise guest who is going to read you a story," she told us. "Please give a warm welcome to my good friend . . . the Tooth Fairy!"

Some big lady came dancing into the

room. She was wearing a yellow tutu, wings, high heels, and a crown on top of her long blond hair. In her hand was a magic wand with a star at the end of it.

Well, I *thought* she was a lady, anyway. She looked a lot like our principal, Mr. Klutz. But he has no hair at all. I mean *none*. Mr. Klutz would look good with long blond hair.

"Hi boys and girls!" the Tooth Fairy said.

The Tooth Fairy *sounded* a lot like Mr. Klutz too.

"You have a pretty low voice for a fairy," I said. "Are you sure you're not Mr. Klutz in disguise?"

"Klutz?" said the Tooth Fairy, adjusting her hair. "Never heard of him. I'm the Tooth Fairy."

"I'm so glad you could join us on National Dessert Day," said Dr. Floss. "Please tell the kids what you do."

"Well," said the Tooth Fairy, "when a kid loses one of their baby teeth and leaves it under their pillow at night, I sneak into their bedroom and replace the lost tooth with money."

I wasn't buying any of that. Neither was anybody else.

"How do you sneak into people's houses?" asked Neil.

"I . . . uh . . . climb in through the chimney," said the Tooth Fairy. "Like Santa Claus. Hey, would you kids like to hear a story?"

"Don't you get dirty climbing through people's chimneys?" asked Ryan.

"What if somebody lives in an apartment building?" asked Michael.

"This is a really fun story," said the Tooth Fairy, taking out a book.

"Isn't it illegal to break into people's houses without permission?" asked Alexia.

"I . . . uh . . . never thought about it,"

admitted the Tooth Fairy. She rubbed her forehead.

"Did anyone ever call the cops on you?" I asked. "Did you ever go to jail?"

"No!" replied the Tooth Fairy. "I just give money to kids when their baby teeth fall out! And by the way, if your tooth is a perfect tooth, I'll give you a dollar. If your tooth is all decayed, I'll only give you a nickel. So take good care of your baby teeth."

Everybody started buzzing, but not really, because we're not bees.

"A nickel?"

"That's *it*?"

"The Tooth Fairy is *cheap*!"

"Hey, the more teeth fall out, the more money I pay," said the Tooth Fairy.

"I might as well knock all my teeth out at once," said Ryan. "Ka-ching!"

"Look, do you kids want to hear the story, or not?" asked the Tooth Fairy.

I was still pretty sure the Tooth Fairy was Mr. Klutz. He started to read us a picture book. . . .

"Once upon a time, there was a little boy who was afraid of going to the dentist and blah blah blah blah blah blah blah blah blah blah blah blah blah blah blah blah blah blah blah . . ."*

---

* That's what it sounds like when grown-ups talk. Nobody knows why.

What a snoozefest. That story went on for a hundred million minutes. I thought I was gonna die from old age. It was about some kid who was afraid of going to the dentist, and on the last page of the story he suddenly gets confident and he's not afraid of going to the dentist anymore.

Gee, what a surprise! Like we couldn't predict *that* was going to happen.

"Hey, I heard that Emily lost a baby tooth today," said the Tooth Fairy. "Emily, will you come up here?"

Emily ran up to the front of the room. The Tooth Fairy leaned forward to give Emily a dollar bill. But that's when the weirdest thing in the history of the world happened. The Tooth Fairy's long blond hair fell off!

The Tooth Fairy was completely bald!

"You *are* Mr. Klutz!" I shouted.

"No, I'm the Tooth Fairy," Mr. Klutz yelled. And then he went running out of the room.

That was weird. And Mr. Klutz is nuts. But he gave me a great idea. There should be a Hair Fairy who sneaks around in the middle of the night giving money to men when their hair falls out. Ka-ching! If there was a Hair Fairy, my dad would be rich.

"Well, that was fun," said Dr. Floss. "I have to go to another class now, but I'll see you kids later, at my favorite time of day."

"When is your favorite time of day?" Andrea asked.

"Two thirty," she said. "Get it? Tooth hurty? That's another dental joke!"

Everybody laughed even though she didn't say anything funny.

Open Wide and Say Ah!

National Dessert Day was winding down. It was almost time for dismissal.

"Okay, *finally* we can get some work done," said Mr. Cooper. "Turn to page twenty-three in your math books."

And you'll never believe who poked her head into the door at that moment.

Nobody! If you poked your head into a

door, you might chip a tooth. And it would hurt. Didn't we go over that in Chapter Three? But you'll never believe who poked her head into the door*way*.

It was Dr. Floss, of course.*

"Is it tooth hurty yet?" she asked. "I mean, two thirty?"

Mr. Cooper rubbed his forehead.

"I have more free stuff to give away!" Dr. Floss announced.

"Yay!" everybody shouted, because everybody loves getting free stuff even though our parents pay for everything anyway.

---

* Anybody could have guessed that. Her picture is right on the cover of the book!

I figured that Dr. Floss would be giving out free skateboards or footballs or something cool like that. But instead, she passed out toothbrushes. Bummer in the summer! She also passed out these teeny tiny tubes of toothpaste. I guess they're for brushing teeny tiny teeth.

"These are just souvenirs," Dr. Floss told us. "Don't brush your teeth with them. Remember, if you brush your teeth, you won't get cavities. And if you don't get cavities, you won't need me. And if you don't need me, I won't be able to buy a new car."

"You're just joking about that, right?" asked Andrea. "You really want us to brush our teeth, don't you?"

"That's for me to know and you to find out," Dr. Floss replied. "But wasn't National Dessert Day fun?"

"Yes!" shouted all the girls.

"No!" shouted all the boys.

"There's just one more thing I need to

do before you kids leave for the day," she told us.

"What?"

"Look in your mouth," she said.

"I can't look in my mouth," I said. "It's part of my head."

"No, I mean *I* need to look in your mouth," said Dr. Floss.

Oh. That's different. Dr. Floss had us all line up. She gave each of us a little tablet to chew on. She said the tablets had

vegetable dye in them so she would be able to see if we have a lot of plaque on our teeth.

"I hope you kids have lots of plaque and some nice cavities," Dr. Floss said as she passed out the tablets. "If you do, I may ask you to come to my office after school today. Tell your moms and dads to bring their checkbooks and credit cards, because it's going to cost them a lot of money. New cars are expensive, you know."

I chewed the tablet. It tasted kind of bitter.

"I've never had a cavity," bragged Andrea, who has to be the best at everything all the time. Dr. Floss said Andrea could go first.

"Open wide and say ah!"

"Ahhh . . ." said Andrea.

Dr. Floss took a little flashlight out of her pocket and looked around in Andrea's mouth with a stick that had a little mirror on the end.

"You have a lovely mouth, Andrea," she said. "No cavities in here, darn it."

"I knew it!" said Andrea.

Dr. Floss gave her a lollipop.

"If you eat enough lollipops," Dr. Floss told Andrea, "you'll get a mouth full of cavities."

No fair! I wanted a lollipop.

Next it was Ryan's turn. Dr. Floss looked in his mouth with the little mirror.

"Ahhh . . ."

"You have a beautiful smile, Ryan," she said, and gave him a lollipop too.

"Thank you!" Ryan said.

Next it was Neil's turn. Dr. Floss looked in his mouth. Then she took out her wallet and pulled out a dollar.

"Here's a dollar," she told Neil as she handed him the bill and a lollipop.

"Thanks!" Neil said. "But why are you

giving me a dollar?"

"Because you have buck teeth!" said Dr. Floss. "Get it? Buck teeth? A dollar? That's a dental joke."

Everybody laughed even though she didn't say anything funny.

Next it was Alexia's turn. Dr. Floss looked in her mouth.

"Ahhh . . ."

"Clean as a whistle. No cavities," Dr. Floss said as she handed Alexia a lollipop. Those lollipops looked good.

Next it was Michael's turn. Dr. Floss looked in his mouth.

"Ahhh . . ."

"No cavities here, darn it!" said Dr. Floss as she gave him a lollipop.

"You kids need to eat more candy and junk food. You don't have any cavities. It looks like I won't be able to buy a new car after all."

After a million hundred minutes, finally it was my turn.

Dr. Floss looked in my mouth.

"Ahhh . . ." I said.

"Hmmmmm," said Dr. Floss.

Hmmmmm? What does hmmmmm mean? I didn't like the sound of hmmmmm. Hmmmmm is a terrible word.

"What is it?" I asked as Dr. Floss looked inside my mouth.

"Hmmmmm," said Dr. Floss again.

Ryan was looking at me. Michael was looking at me. Andrea was looking at me. *Everybody* was looking at me. Nobody was saying anything. It was so quiet, you could hear a pin drop. That is, if anybody had pins with them. But why would you bring pins to school? That would be weird.

"A.J.," Dr. Floss finally said, "can you ask your mom or dad to bring you to my office after school today?" She handed me a business card.

"NOOOOOOOOOOOOOO!" I shouted. "I don't want to die!"

"Don't be silly," said Dr. Floss. "I just want to examine your teeth a little more carefully."

"Well . . . okay," I agreed reluctantly. "Can I have a lollipop?"

"I think you've had too many lollipops already, A.J.," said Dr. Floss.

It wasn't fair! I was going to die, and I didn't even get a lollipop. This was the worst day of my life.

Good News and Bad News

When my mom picked me up after school, I gave her the business card and told her what Dr. Floss said.

"This could be an emergency," my mom said as she hit the gas. "Let's go to her office right now!"

This was the worst thing to happen since TV Turnoff Week! I wanted to go to

Antarctica and live with the penguins. I'll bet a million hundred dollars that penguins never have to go to the dentist.

But I'm no dummy. I reached into the back seat of the car and put on my football helmet.

"A.J., why are you wearing your football helmet?" Mom asked me. "The dentist won't be able to get into your mouth with that face guard in the way."

"Exactly," I said.

It didn't take long to drive to Dr. Floss's office. Mom made me leave my football helmet in the car. That's when the weirdest thing in the history of the world happened.

When we walked into the waiting room, there was a bowl of candy on the table. And a bunch of cool toys. And a video game system hooked up to a big-screen TV!

It was paradise.

"This place is cool," I told my mom. "Can I live here?"

Mom said I could play a video game while she talked with the receptionist. I told her to take all the time she needed. I was just about to press the START button when—

"Dr. Floss will see you now, A.J.," said the receptionist.

Bummer in the summer!

"I'll be right here waiting for you," my mother told me.

"Come in with me, Mom," I said. "I'm scared."

"You're a big boy," she replied. "I'll be right here when you're done."

The receptionist walked me down a long hallway. I felt like one of those prisoners being taken to jail. Finally we got to a little room. Dr. Floss was in there.

"Hi A.J.!" she said cheerfully. "It's nice to see you again."

I looked around the room. It was *scary*. There was a dentist chair with a big light hanging over it, and all kinds of dentist tools. Then I looked on the windowsill. There were a bunch of pliers lined up there.

"AHHHHHHHH!" I shouted. "Is that what you use to pull out people's teeth?"

"Oh no, that's my collection of antique pliers," Dr. Floss said. "Remember this morning I told you that I collect old tools?"

Oh yeah. I looked around the office some more. In the corner, leaning against the wall, was a giant jackhammer.

"AHHHHHHHH!" I shouted. I thought I was gonna die. "Is that what you use to

drill people's teeth?"

"Of course not!" said Dr. Floss. "Remember this morning I told you I like doing roadwork?"

"I thought that meant you like to go jogging."

"No, silly," she told me. "In my spare time, I work on the roads."

That's weird. Well, at least she wasn't going to stick that thing in my mouth.

"Take a look at *this*, A.J.," she said, holding up a set of teeth and gums. Then suddenly the teeth started chattering.

"Cool," I said. "What do you call that?"

"My last patient," replied Dr. Floss.

"AHHHHHHHH!" I shouted.

"Just kidding!" said Dr. Floss. "You're so jumpy, A.J."

"I don't like going to the dentist," I admitted.

"There's nothing to be afraid of," she told me. "Here, sit in the chair. It's really comfortable."

I sat in the big chair, and it *was* comfortable. That's when the weirdest thing in the history of the world happened. Dr. Floss pulled a seat belt across my waist and clicked it shut.

"AHHHHHHHH!" I shouted. "What are you doing?"

"You should always wear your seat belt," she told me.

"That's in a car!" I shouted. "Mom! Help! Get me out of here!"

"Just relax, A.J.," Dr. Floss told me.

It was probably a soundproof room. That way, the parents in the waiting room can't hear Dr. Floss torturing kids.

She pushed a secret button to lean the chair back. I was looking at the ceiling now. And you'll never guess in a million hundred years what Dr. Floss had up on the ceiling.

It was a TV screen! Cool! There was some cartoon playing on the TV.

Dr. Floss put on a pair of rubber gloves.

"AHHHHHHHH!" I shouted. "Not the gloves!"

In the movies, bad guys always put on gloves before they steal something or murder somebody. That way, they don't leave fingerprints behind.

"Shhhh," she said, sticking the big light in my face. "You just watch the cartoon while I look inside your mouth, A.J. Open wide."

"No," I said.

"A.J., I can't work on your teeth if you don't open your mouth."

"I know," I told her. "That's why I'm not opening it."

"Don't be a baby, A.J. You probably just have one tiny cavity. Open up."

"No!"

If I didn't open my mouth, Dr. Floss couldn't look inside it. And if she couldn't look inside it, she couldn't examine me. And if she couldn't examine me, she wouldn't know for sure if I had a cavity. And if she didn't know for sure if I had a cavity, she couldn't drill my teeth. So I wasn't going to open my mouth.

"Here," she said, handing me a rubber

ball. "Squeeze this stress ball. It will help you relax."

I squeezed the stress ball but felt just as much stress as I did before. I kept my mouth shut and crossed my arms in front of my chest. When you cross your arms in front of your chest, it means you're not going to do what somebody wants you to do. That's the first rule of being a kid.

"Well," said Dr. Floss with a sigh, "I guess I'm just going to have to pull out *all* your teeth, just to be on the safe side."

"WHAT?!"

While I was saying "WHAT," Dr. Floss grabbed my upper and lower teeth and pulled them apart.

"Dr. Floss is the boss!" she said, peering into my mouth. "Say ah."

"Ahhhhhhhhh," I said.

Dr. Floss whistled while she looked around inside my mouth.

"What kind of car are you going to buy?" I asked.

"Oh, it depends," she replied. "If you have a lot of cavities, I'll buy a limousine. But if you only have one tiny cavity, I'll probably get a little . . . hmmmmm."

Hmmmmm? Not hmmmmm again! That can't be good.

"What do you see?" I asked.

"Not enough," replied Dr. Floss. "I'm going to shoot an X-ray to help me see better."

"What's that?" I asked.

"It's a picture of your tooth," she told me. "I call them tooth pics. Get it? Tooth pics? Toothpicks? That's a little dental joke."

I didn't laugh. Her jokes were terrible.

Dr. Floss took something out of a drawer.

"Here," she said, "bite down on this cookie."

Cookies?! I *love* cookies! I opened my mouth and bit down.

It wasn't a cookie! It was some yucky plastic thing! I thought I was gonna throw up.

"Just keep biting down," Dr. Floss told me. "Sit still. I'll be in the next room for a moment."

"Are X-rays dangerous?" I mumbled, keeping that thing in my teeth.

"There's nothing to worry about," she said as she left the room. "X-rays are harmless."

"Then why are you hiding in the next room?" I mumbled.

Dr. Floss didn't answer. There was a little beep, and she came back and took the plastic thing out of my mouth. Then she put it in a machine for a few minutes. The machine must have developed the X-ray, because she put it up on a box with a light in it and I could see a picture of my teeth. Dr. Floss looked at it for like a million hundred seconds.

"A.J.," she finally said. "I have some good

news and some bad news."

Uh-oh. Any time a grown-up tells you they have good news and bad news, the news is always bad. That's the first rule of being a grown-up.

"What's the good news?" I asked.

"I'm not going to tell you."

"WHAT?!"

"Okay, okay, I'll tell you," Dr. Floss said. "But you have to read the next chapter. So nah nah nah boo boo on you."*

---

* Hey, I thought I was supposed to say that! And how did she know there were chapters?

Swish and Spit

"Okay," I said after we started the new chapter, "what's the good news?"

"The good news," Dr. Floss replied, "is that an elephant is *not* going to charge in here and sit on you."

What?! That's good news? It never even occurred to me that an elephant would sit on me.

"What's the bad news?" I asked.

"As I suspected," said Dr. Floss, "one of your teeth has a tiny cavity in it."

"NOOOOOOOOOOOOOOO!" I shrieked. "Not that! My life is over!"

"One little cavity isn't a big deal, A.J.," she told me. "I can fix that in a jiffy."

"You're going to put my tooth in peanut butter?" I asked.

"No, silly," she told me. "I'll clean out the cavity and put a filling in the tooth to fill the hole."

"NOOOOOOOOOOOO!" I shouted. That sounded *horrible*. I tried to make a run for it, but the seat belt held me back.

"Lots of kids are afraid of the dentist," Dr. Floss told me, pulling something out of her drawer. "But I know just the thing that will help you, A.J. Let me just put this mask on."

"NOOOOOOOOOOO!" I shouted. "Murderers always wear masks!"

"*You* wear the mask," she said putting this clear plastic thing over my nose. "This will relax you."

"What is it?" I asked.

"I'm going to give you some nitrous oxide," Dr. Floss replied.

That sounded scary.

"Don't be frightened," Dr. Floss said. "It's called laughing gas."

Laughing gas, eh? Well, *I'm* not going to laugh.

No way.

Nobody tells *me* when to laugh.

I felt a little weird.

"Ha-ha-ha-ha-ha-ha-ha-ha-ha-ha-ha! Ha-ha-ha-ha-ha-ha-ha-ha-ha-ha-ha! Ha-ha-ha-ha-ha-ha-ha-ha-ha-ha-ha! Ha-ha-ha-ha-ha-ha-ha-ha-ha-ha-ha! Ha-ha-ha-ha-ha-ha-ha-ha-ha-ha-ha! Ha-ha-ha-ha-! Ha-ha-ha-ha-ha-ha-ha-ha-

ha-ha-ha-ha-ha-ha-ha!"*

"Okay," said Dr. Floss, sticking this curvy metal thing into my mouth. "It's time for Mr. Thirsty, the sucking question mark."

"Not Mr. Thirsty!" I shouted. "Ha-ha-ha-ha-ha-ha-ha-ha!"

"You're doing fine, A.J.," said Dr. Floss. "Now I just need to drill into that cavity a little."

---

* In case you were wondering, that's me laughing.

"Not the drill!" I shouted. "Ha-ha-ha-ha-ha-ha-ha-help!"

Dr. Floss stuck something in my mouth that buzzed and vibrated my whole head. It felt weird, but it didn't hurt. Actually it was kind of fun.

"Now I'm going to put the filling in," Dr. Floss told me.

"Can I have chocolate filling?" I asked. "Ha-ha-ha-ha-ha-ha-ha-ha!"

"We're just about done, A.J.," she said.

"Ha-ha-ha-ha-ha-ha-ha-ha-ha!" I said. "Take your time."

A few seconds later, she took the mask off my face.

"You did *great*, A.J.!" said Dr. Floss. "Now take a swig from this cup of green water and spit it into the little sink."

"Green water?" I asked. "Gross! How did it get green?"

"You ask too many questions," said Dr. Floss. "Don't drink it. Just swish and spit!"

I swished and spit.

"Can you put that mask back on me again?" I asked.

"No, we're all done, A.J.," Dr. Floss told me. "That tooth is as good as new. Now remember, keep eating lots of candy, cakes, and chocolate, and drinking sugary soft drinks, because I want to see you back here again real soon."

I went out to the waiting room. My mother was there, playing video games. Not fair!

"How did my little boy do?" she asked.

"He was very brave," Dr. Floss told her.

My mom gave the receptionist her credit card. As we were about to walk out the door, Dr. Floss came running over.

"Oh, A.J., I forgot something," she said.

Oh no. What was she going to do to me *now*?

"Have a lollipop," said Dr. Floss.

Well, that's pretty much what happened. Maybe Dr. Floss will get a new car. Maybe we'll figure out how to bring headlights to school. Maybe Captain Plaque and Fluoride will fight again. Maybe Mr. Klutz will stop wearing a tutu and a blond wig. Maybe I'll start a collection of teeny tiny toothpaste tubes. Maybe Ryan will knock out all his teeth and get rich. Maybe Dr. Floss will stop making bad dentist jokes. Maybe we'll finally get through page twenty-three in our math books.

But it won't be easy!